It's Time

It's Time for a Haircut

Cathryn Summers

illustrated by
Aurora Aguilera

PowerKiDS
press.

New York

Published in 2018 by The Rosen Publishing Group, Inc.
29 East 21st Street, New York, NY 10010

First Edition

Managing Editor: Nathalie Beullens-Maoui
Editor: Elizabeth Krajnik
Art Director: Michael Flynn
Book Design: Raúl Rodriguez
Illustrator: Aurora Aguilera

Cataloging-in-Publication Data

Names: Summers, Cathryn, author.
Title: It's time for a haircut / Cathryn Summers.
Other titles: It is time for a haircut
Description: New York : PowerKids Press, [2018] | Series: It's time |
  Includes index.
Identifiers: LCCN 2017013093| ISBN 9781538327319 (pbk. book) | ISBN
  9781538327623 (6 pack) | ISBN 9781508163664 (library bound book)
Subjects: LCSH: Haircutting–Juvenile literature.
Classification: LCC TT970 .S86 2018 | DDC 646.7/24–dc23
LC record available at https://lccn.loc.gov/2017013093

Manufactured in the United States of America

CPSIA Compliance Information: Batch #BW18PK. For further information contact Rosen Publishing, New York, New York at 1-800-237-9932

Parent
picture
Summ

Contents

Today is a special day.
I'm going to get my first haircut!

My dad and I drive to the barbershop.

The barber cuts my dad's hair first.

There are a lot
of men in the
barbershop.

8

They talk to each other.

Now it's my turn. I'm very excited
for my haircut!

First, the barber uses scissors.

He cuts off lots of hair.

12

I like to see my hair drop on the floor. My hair is going to be short!

Next, the barber uses the clippers.

These cut my hair very short.

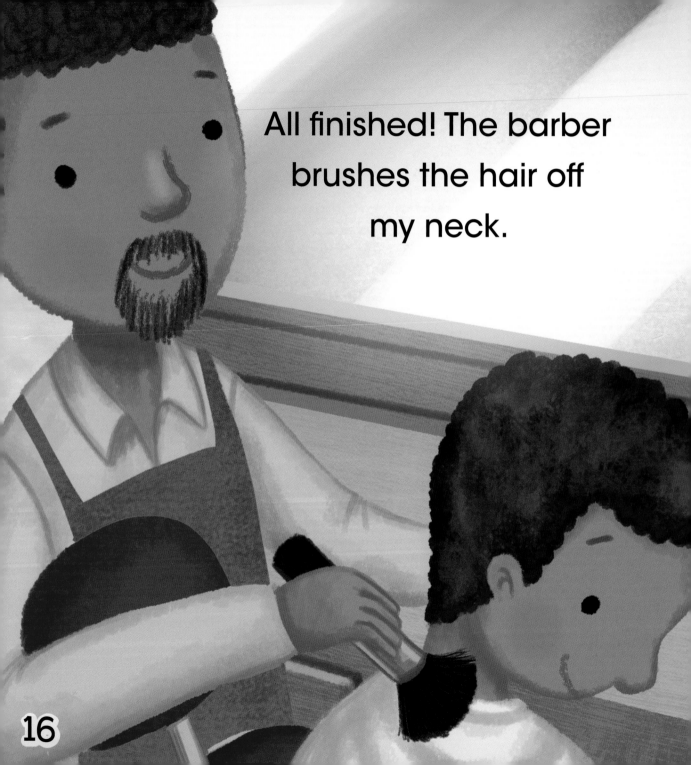

All finished! The barber brushes the hair off my neck.

16

Wow! My haircut looks great!
I say thank you to the barber.

My dad pays the barber.

My mom loves my haircut.

I can't wait for the
next one!

23

Words to Know

barber

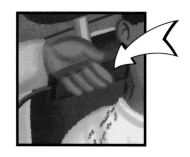
clippers

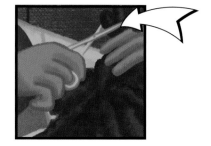
scissors

Index

24